IMPENETRABLE FALSEHOODS
A Small Book of Small Fiction

ଔ

Early Praise for *Impenetrable Falsehoods*

ଔ

"I really love this. It drew me in with stories that you inhabit instead of visit."

~ The Squeaky Wheel Blog

"I found myself noticing prose for the first time in a long time. The descriptions here are wonderfully effective, creating an atmosphere I could sec, hear, smell..."

~ Elle Todd, author of *The Elect*

"E.W. Storch weaves together a spellbinding collection of stories that captivate, entertain, and leave you wishing for more."

~ Stephanie Ayers, author of *Til Death Do Us Part*

Impenetrable Falsehoods

A Small Book of Small Fiction

E.W. Storch

ALL CAPS PUBLISHING

ISBN-13: 978-0615888590

ISBN-10: 0615888593

ALL CAPS PUBLISHING
P.O. Box 368
Easthampton, MA 01027
Visit the publisher's website at:
http://www.allcapspublishing.com
Or email:
info@allcapspublishing.com

Visit the author's website at:
http://sinistralscribblings.wordpress.com

For Tracey,
whose patience, understanding, and love
have been my bulwark during dark times.
She also makes a mean lasagna.

ଓଃଡ

ꕥ

Contents

ꕥ

My stone is small and fixed,
It runs the scope of language.
A channel of faded letters,
Through which my imagination comes alive.

ଔଷ

Introduction

They say that one of the best ways to start a speech is with a joke. Well, this introduction isn't quite a speech, but I think most of us are familiar with the joke about the World's Oldest Profession. I have to disagree with that assertion. I believe the World's Oldest Profession is storytelling.

Storytelling was one of the first skills developed by humans in prehistory. It was used to teach and explain things that had no explanation, such as how the earth, sun, moon and stars came to be. It was used to explain changes in weather and strange aspects of nature. Stories were told to explain the human condition, and we wove tales of infidelity, thievery and heroism.

Stories were told to entertain and educate.

We know many of these ancient stories today. We may not know them in their primal spoken form, but we do have written accounts of them. The mythologies of ancient cultures are familiar to us; those of the Norse, Greeks, Romans, Welsh, the Far and Near East. These stories are rich with plot and interesting characters, fantastic places and events and themes.

True storytellers are a rare breed. Anyone can tell a

story, but I think there are two things that you really must have to be good at it: you must be a good reader, and you must be a good liar.

A good reader is someone who will read anything and everything. It doesn't matter what it is. A good reader is someone who will digest a book, learning about plot, theme, style and story. He or she observes how authors write to achieve different effects or emotional responses, while also paying attention to grammar and syntax. The good reader then remembers all these things, storing away that information to save it for analysis.

A good liar is someone who can weave a simple, yet impenetrable, falsehood with nobody the wiser. A very good liar can spin a yarn so well that he or she can then add to it with ease and without complicating matters. In essence, a good liar is an on-the-fly storyteller. If you're a good liar, all you need to be a storyteller is the knowledge you get from being a good reader. The reverse is also true.

You don't need a pretty piece of paper that says nothing more than you spent tens of thousands of dollars on an institution of higher learning to be a good storyteller. You don't need to attend creative writing seminars.

To be a good wordsmith, you just need to be able to read well and lie well. I think my mother can attest to how well (and often) I lied when I was young and, if my personal library says nothing else, it does say I read a lot.

The book you hold in your hands is my attempt to entertain and enlighten with my own brand of storytelling. It is a compilation of both some of the best stories from, and inspired by, my web-log, Sinistral Scribblings, as well as never before seen work. All of these stories have been revised to varying degrees and are presented here in the form that I originally intended, free from the constraints of blogging. They explore love, death, war, the supernatural and the just plain weird.

Rural New Hampshire, October, 2013

Journal Entry: June 10, 2009

Today, I thought about goals. Short-term and long-term. I was playing Guild Wars—as I do every morning—and realized that I set myself a goal to accomplish every day in the game. They are small goals, taking no more than an hour or two, but they are goals I complete every single day. It got me thinking. "Why do I do this? Because it's easy and fun. Well, why can't I attempt harder and more meaningful goals?"

I immediately thought of writing.

If I can dedicate some time every day to writing as I do a video game, might I succeed? Surely.

So here I sit, with a little notebook, listening to Miles Davis—jazz is the best for writing in my opinion—with my hand already cramping from years of disuse.

What do I write about?

☙❧

Memory as a Carousel

This time, I'm five years old. I don't even need to get my bearings this go-round. In an instant, I know this is Christmas day at my grandmother's house. My senses are assaulted by the noise of a happy family, smells of Christmas dinner and stale cigarettes. Before me lies a large gift, my name carefully written on the tag. I know it's the first of many LEGO sets that will give me years of fun-filled rainy days.

Just on the other side of the tree is my brother, only three, still showing the signs of retained baby fat. He smiles gleefully as he tears the paper from a box. My grandmother has maneuvered herself by my side and kisses me wetly on the cheek, smelling like whiskey and a dirty ashtray. I rub the slime away and reach for the present…

Shift.

The room is dark and barely lit by a half-moon. There are arms wrapped around me, a mouth firmly planted on mine, tongues fencing in the heat. All I can smell is her shampoo and perfume, mixed with the garlic and wet dog smells of the house. One of my hands is tangled in hair, the other groping under a sweater trying to clumsily undo the clasp on a bra. She is grinding her hips into my lap, moaning, asking for more. My arousal is painful because it has nowhere to go in my tight jeans.

Seventeen then.

All of my virgin fears hit me in an instant. Never before have I done what she asks of me. She makes a frustrated sound, pushes me back onto the couch. She pulls her sweater off and my eyes fixate on the space between her white, blue-veined breasts. Reaching behind her, she releases the clasp and lets her bra fall…

Shift.

Bright lights nearly blind me after being in the dark room. I stumble a few steps, loose-fitting shoes flopping on the floor. A large room surrounds me, industrial lighting leaving no shadowed corners. Stainless steel tables and benches are bolted to the floor and a number of men are about, sitting or standing wearing orange jumpsuits. Looking down, I am wearing the same jumpsuit and lace-less sneakers.

I am twenty.

On the table next to me is a box of tobacco and rolling papers. Expertly, I roll a cigarette, not noticing the two men watching me with unblinking eyes. In the far wall is a mesh covered heating element, used only for lighting cigarettes. I push the button, the coils glow like an ember and I lean in to light the twig.

My arms are grabbed at the wrists and twisted behind me while a rough hand shoves my face into the mesh covering…

Shift.

Today I am twenty-seven and I stand on a sidewalk, *Unter den Linden* stretching before me, the Brandenburg Gate at my back.

Shift.

Twenty-five, full of booze and pot, a guitar in my hands, fingers working furiously, hair in my face, drums beating the funky rhythms of Jimi Hendrix.

Shift.

Eighteen, staring into the empty dorm room, gleeful that I'm finally going to be out from under my parent's iron boot heels.

Shift.

Minneapolis's hallucinogenic nights.

Shift.

Orlando and marching feet.

Shift.

Chopping off dreadlocks in Plattsburgh.

Shift.

A Richmond bus station.

Shift, shift, shift.

It blurs now, an ever-increasing slide show of everything I have ever seen or done. There is no set pattern of what shifts to when. Time has no meaning. Details have no meaning. Experiences I enjoyed last mere seconds, while agonizing heartaches last forever.

I spin on and on, a passenger on my own tour bus, not knowing when this masochistic carousel is going to stop.

I ride it, though, because I know that when it does stop, I will experience sights, sounds, smells and characters to draw from for my next lie.

ଔ୭

Martyrs & Stained Glass

"Forgive me, for I have sinned," he prayed. "She made me know who I am."

The cathedral echoed his whispered words in a voicelessness that floated along the arched ceiling. Candles provided a lonely illumination at floor level. The vast space above was an infinite blackness, filled only by his guilt-ridden words.

The stained glass mosaic behind the altar was back-lit, the Virgin holding the baby Christ for a phantom congregation. Saint Joseph, the patron of the cathedral, looked up with longing while the Archangel Michael stood quietly to the side, spear in hand, vigilant.

He always thought it a strange portrayal of the Birth, but never spent much time looking at the window. He was usually on the other side of the altar, the window behind him. The archangel seemed to be staring accusation right through him.

"She hurt and she suffered," he whispered, pleading to the glass angel. "The cancer was terminal and she asked only the touch of another before she enters your Kingdom."

The angel remained impassive and the baby smiled with innocent joy.

A small cry punched from his throat and tears came unbidden, rolling down his cheeks, wetting his stiff collar, the symbol of his vocation.

"You teach us to succor the sick," he sobbed, pressing his forehead into his clasped hands. "She was young, so young, and lamented the short time she had to enjoy your creation." His head rose and he pleaded to the Virgin, "She only wanted to know what it was like before she would be gone forever—and she chose me, your servant, to aid her."

He lowered his head again, waited while his echoed voice died among the dark arches.

"And yet, you make us, who wear the cloth, live a life of abstinence. A life devoid of these simple, beautiful, human experiences that you gave to us in Paradise!" The words were sharp, the reverential tone gone. "I have long questioned in my heart your plans for me. I look at this world and witness suffering and hate, death and war. I see my fellow man sinking farther and farther into the abyss past the point of no return."

He pounded his hands on the altar rail. "And where are you?" His voice growled in darkness. "How can you let these things happen? How can you say to me that what I did was wrong? That an experience of happiness is denied when it can counter all the evil being wrought?" He shook his head. "I gave her what she wanted in her last hours. She was happy. She felt joy." His breath came slow and even, calming. "And so did I."

He stood, slowly unfolding himself, defiant, clenched hands at his sides, head high. "It doesn't make sense. Why deny someone who has walked in your light all their life what they want in their last hours? She and I gave to each other that night and we took from each other."

He nodded once, a decision made. He grasped the stiff collar encircling his neck and tore the cassock off. He held it loosely before him and studied it with intent.

"This was a symbol of what I thought you wanted from me. A symbol of how I intended to serve your Will." He turned his hand, letting the cassock fall to the floor before the altar. "No more."

He turned and walked up the aisle. After a few steps he stopped and whispered over his shoulder, "I will serve you without the restriction of the collar. Maybe that's the way it's supposed to be."

ᘓᘐ

The Road

Most of the trees had already lost their leaves. The drive up Interstate 87 had become a funeral procession, the trees dressed in their best grays and blacks. Even the sky was depressed; at any moment it would start shedding tears for the lost ones. Sometime in the past eight years, the speed limit had changed from 55 to 65, but the traffic didn't move any faster. The unspoken law was that everyone drove 80 miles an hour anyway.

Whoosh! The skeletal trees blur past.

It was a short drive from Albany to Saratoga. Only half an hour if you drove with the traffic; longer if you obeyed the speed limit. The radio was playing an old rock tune, the kind about lost love with a bouncy beat. Fingers tap the steering wheel.

New York is a beautiful state no matter where you are. Traveling north towards the Adirondacks is the best country, though, especially in the autumn. The mountains blaze with flames of trees, fiery colors glowing in the sunlight. By November, the flames have been extinguished, leaving the charred, dead remains behind. It was so now, traveling to

Saratoga, the native land burned clean of all life.

The funeral was in two days. Thanksgiving in three. The phone call had come last night at one in the morning. The voice forced the news through choked tears. Your Grandmother has passed away, it said, won't you come home? The funeral is in two days. Grandpa wants you to be a pallbearer. Please stay for Thanksgiving. The receiver silently slipped back into the cradle.

It wasn't a surprise to anyone. Grandma had been slowly dying in the nursing home. Actually, the family was surprised she had lasted as long as she did. What was it Uncle Larry used to say? "She's a tough old broad, the Queen Mother. Slavic," and he would nod, as if that one word explained everything about her. Grandma was tough: the best.

So, bags were packed, the wife was kissed goodbye. "Are you going to be okay, honey?" A nod, another kiss and a question. "No, I'll stay here with the kids. Call me when you get there." Another kiss. The car starts and the rising sun follows, blazing in the rear-view mirror. New Hampshire and the life carefully built there is left behind.

Whoosh! The blurring trees.

Pit stop in Albany, the call of Nature.

Coffee.

Back on the road.

Eight years was a long time.

The radio shouts the morning traffic report. A glance out the side window confirms the news. The Interstate is busy. More music. A touch of a button silences the noise.

Memories flood back on the drive. A smile, a kind word. The smell of freshly made dill pickles in a jar on the back porch. The feel of the newly tilled earth underfoot as a vegetable garden is planted. The musty smells of the shed where last year's onions and potatoes are kept. Soap bubbles floating down to a close-cropped lawn as laughing children chase them, popping them on their stubby fingers. Grilled cheese sandwiches and warm Coke. And everywhere, always, she is there, laughing and playing, enjoying life. Happy to be a part of a family.

She had always been there. She wasn't ever supposed to leave. What went wrong?

A sign blares white on green, "Exit 16, One Mile." Almost there. Guts start to turn upside down and sweaty palms lose grip on the wheel. The exit approaches and the click-click of the turn signal sounds like the snip-snip of the shears she used to trim the hedges an eternity ago.

Slow down. Turn left.

The truck stop hasn't changed at all. Huge, beastly machines crouch, rumbling, growling and roaring, spewing out blackness; covering the sky in a blanket of fumes. Worn out, wrinkled, dirty men walk to and from the restaurant, skinny legs barely holding up beach ball sized stomachs. A sea of ball caps, brims bent into half-circles scream out philosophies of the road: *He who dies with the most toys wins*, *FORD--Fix Or Repair Daily*, *I'd rather be fishin'*.

In an instant, the truck stop is past and a sad church can be seen, sagging, losing paint with tall dead weeds in the lot. A sign by the road reads,

The Lord is my
hepard,
I sh ll not wan .
oday's h mns:

A pastor stands out front sweeping the leaves from the steps that lead to the sanctuary; a sad sagging man, black coat hung over scant shoulders, who glances up at the road as the cars go past. The church, the sign and the pastor shrink in the rear view mirror.

Turn left again and the produce store, closed for the season, disappears as corn fields approach, empty and barren, except for the neat rows of beige corn stumps, bent over from the harvest. The road follows the hilly country, miles of empty fields marked occasionally by tumbled down stone walls and solitary trees that can still vaguely remember a time when the native people roamed, free to walk the forests of a still untouched land. Through the haze of distance, a thick forest can be seen, a silent sentinel at the far end of the fields that looks as if at any moment it will start a slow plodding trek to retake them and again call the land home.

The road continues on and memories of hot summer days surface, riding bicycles as fast as possible, the breeze cooling sweat that drips down the sides of smiling faces. Skidding to a stop in the dirt of the produce store lot, the dust settles onto the moistness of those faces. Coolness and the smell of freshly cut pine boards greet the dirt-smeared grins. Grubby hands grab at candy fishes and pennies are tossed on the counter as the woman reaches for the money, hands and face prematurely aged by years of farm labor. She smiles and yells to be careful. Back into the heat, the bicycles head home.

Back to the car as it heads home.

Home is always two places. First, it is the place where life begins, a childhood lived; a place where all the firsts of life occur. It is the place you remember in your dreams and the place you remember most clearly when watching your own children.

The second home is where your children experience all of their firsts. Even if it is the same house, it has become a second home because all the firsts you have lived can never be lived again. You may watch your children take their first steps, say their first word, learn to ride a bicycle, drive a car, hear them talk of their first kiss in hushed tones while they're on the phone, and for a moment, a single fleeting moment, you may come as close to reliving your past as possible before the sadness and emptiness fill in that place for something missed but dearly cherished.

Driving back to the first home.

The forest at the far end of the cornfields has wrapped itself around and become a blockade in the road. The cold, gray-black wall steadily grows larger: the gate to Dante's Inferno, *Abandon all hope ye who enter here*. The trees seem to reach toward the road menacingly, long crooked fingers scraping the wind, searching for the hapless victim who would be forced to listen to their mournful song.

The road leads straight into the trees, undaunted, as proud and arrogant as the self-titled demigod who created it.

The first few trees of the wood speed by and a pall permeates the air. The menacing feeling of the forest is replaced by a melancholy sadness that drips from every branch once the car has entered.

The car slows.

A push of a button and music. Jethro Tull's "Songs From the Wood." The irony: a smirk. The music stops abruptly with another touch of a button.

Houses come now: white, green, blue, brown, yellow: all the colors of the rainbow look foreign on the large blocks built by the same demigod who built the road. The trees closest to the houses weep the most, melancholy puddles at their roots.

It is through the forest, along the road that does not belong, past the houses that do not belong, that the car goes.

Slowly now.

Almost home.

Turn.

There's the drive. Turn again.

Cars parked on the slanting hill. New York license plates. Massachusetts license plates.

Pull the car in, park. Turn the ignition, pull the key, sigh.

Mom, I'm home.

☙❧

Mirror

The doppelganger stares balefully
Beyond the polished glass,
Sunken azure eyes
Bleeding pain and ennui.
Creases fine and deep
Map the hills and valleys
Of a visage once full
Of life and laughter.
At once familiar and foreign,
Young and old,
The mimic admonishes what was
What should have been
What could be.
What was—a young face
Filled with hope,
Promise,
Dreams.
What should have been—the father's face
Confidence,
Knowledge,

Wisdom.
What could be—an amalgam
Dreams, promise, and hope
Birth confidence, knowledge, and wisdom.
Somewhen, a step was missed,
A stair skipped,
The boy and man now
Forever out of phase.
Rage, hate, loathing, and fear
Pushed into the glass,
The father's face stares back
Reflecting blame to the self.
Percolations of emotion
Eye twitch, curled lip, baring teeth
Perceived truth becomes a definition
For years of life.
It is nobody's fault
But mine.

Eulogy

The kitchen sink was in the woods. Not the little brushed steel one that's in the house, but the big, stone one that my dad and my uncle took out of the old Goffe farmhouse. They put it out back, beyond the field and into the woods, carefully choosing a spot by the brook. They tipped it on its side, propped it up with rocks so that it wouldn't right itself and left it there for me and my brother to play in.

Play in it we did. My dad and uncle faced the open side to the brook and my brother and I would sit in it, side by side, listening to the water burble over the moss-slimed rocks. The sink was huge and we could lay in it, stretched out along its length and neither feet nor head would touch the ends.

For many summers, that sink was our fort, our submarine, our house, fishing hut, airplane. It was our getaway place when we needed time alone from the world of adults and make believe called to us. It was a thinking place, and when we were older, it was a make out place.

I write this sitting in my kitchen sink. A kitchen sink that has meant more to me than any other object, even more than some people have.

The sunlight slants in from the right, past the hanging creepers and vines that have invaded my sacred place. It is crusted with a layer of detritus: dead leaves, dirt, animal droppings and sticks. Its old slate gray color has been subsumed by sickly greens and dead grays. The sink looks and smells like a tomb. Its old comfort is gone.

I write this sitting in our kitchen sink. Ours. Mine and my brother's. I pause and listen to the brook, swollen with spring thaw, and can hear it calling out to him. I hear his name whispered upon the mossy rocks. I hear it in the whistle of wind in budded branches. I hear it in the rustle of dried leaves.

I'm sitting in my old spot, left of center, as if he is still here. If I close my eyes, I can feel his body, in that way that you do when someone is near, a faint yet intent electric pulsing. Perhaps he is, I don't know. I never put much stock in ghosts or spirits. He believed in them, though. He loved ghost stories.

The scream of a jay brings back the day when we talked about girls for the first time with any seriousness. He wanted to know if what he had heard about the mechanics of making love was true. Maybe I should have been honest with him, but I was the big brother and bragging wasn't just my job, it was expected. Poor Patricia Wilson suffered from his misplaced deviance. A friend of his soon set him straight, but he gained a reputation in school from it that became the initial crack in a schism that separated us for years.

I never meant for any of that to happen. I thought that maybe, if he would listen to me, accept my apology, that he would be okay. Instead, I took too long.

I waited too long.

I've been staring at the trees, listening to the forest sounds for forty-five minutes. The seat of my pants is wet from the dampness, but not as wet as my eyes. I ask for forgiveness one last time.

ଓଃ

Journal Entry: July 14, 2009

Strangitude. The word grabs at me and I feel compelled to write about it.

I've been revisiting Borges and Delany again, though I feel any attempts to emulate them will fall too flat and appear absurd and confusing rather than the art piece I intend.

Philosophy and metaphysics are strange things and only true to the mind thinking of them.

I'm listening to Bach's Cello Suites for solo Cello. There's a mathematical precision to Bach's works that I find relaxing. It's almost as if Bach had found the mathematics that underlie the foundation of the universe—existence itself—and translated it to music.

My hand stopped while I listened, though my mind continued to go. It arrived at the "Blue Note." That elusive sound or tone that jazz musicians have searched for for decades. A note between the notes. I have often thought it akin to searching for God—or a higher presence—and maybe someone will find the true Blue Note someday.

I find myself questioning and examining my own belief system lately. Not in a search for God, but because there is still much out there that is unexplained. *Déjà vu* is something that has always fascinated me and try as I might, I cannot find a reason for it. In fact, I can explain it many ways.

My hand doesn't move as fast as my brain and I wish I could explain myself more clearly, but by the time I've jotted an idea, my mind has gone through the explanations and is on to the next idea.

Like true *déjà vu*, my explanations have vaporized. I need a voice recorder.

☙❧

"Buddy"

A stranger was in my regular seat at the diner, hunched and alone. He sat at the end of the counter, a cup of coffee between his hands. His dejected posture and vacant stare spoke volumes, so I just shrugged at Rosie rather than make the man change seats. The only free seat was next to him and I took it.

The regular crowd was in, packing the place. Rosie was busy with pouring coffee, serving pies and shouting orders to Rex while he tried his best not to sweat into whatever slop he had going on the grill. Marge was waiting tables, six months pregnant. She didn't have a hard time navigating tables, the guys moved out of her way, chairs constantly scraping as they shifted. Not like in a white-only joint. We respect our women in Harlem.

I took a few moments to study the man I sat next to. It looked as if he hadn't touched his coffee and the hands wrapped around the cup were cracked and dry, a working man's hands. His head hung down, like a ripe melon bursting out of the neck of his tattered coat. His hat was crumpled and sat askew, revealing hair gone to gray. Wrinkles lined his face, overemphasizing the width of his nose and mouth. He was an ugly man, old and worn, like his coat, but I thought I could sense a vibrancy in him.

Rex shouted to Rosie to change the station. Most of the guys at the counter stopped shoveling pie in their faces long enough to watch Rosie stretch up to the radio, her breasts nicely outlined when her uniform pulled tight. Did I say we respect our women in Harlem? Sure do, but that don't mean we can't appreciate the view.

Rosie put on WJZZ and Clifford Brown's trumpet filled the diner, a song from a few years back.

That's how it was that morning of June 27, 1956, the day jazz died and I became a new man.

"That was the great Clifford Brown and Max Roach," the radio man said when the song ended, "with 'The Blues Walk' from their first duo album. We'll be playing Clifford Brown all day, cats, God rest his soul."

Half the diner erupted in questions then, myself among them. What happened? Clifford Brown died yesterday, someone said. A car crash on the way to Chicago.

"Here's to Brownie," someone in back yelled, "Best trumpet player ever to blow the horn!"

Many cheered and raised their mugs, but another voice countered, "My ass! Miles Davis is the best ever."

The other side of the diner erupted into an argument then, one side chest thumping "bop," the other "cool."

Me, I just said a silent prayer for Clifford and tried to listen to the radio.

"He threw it away, y'know," the man next to me said. His voice was that kind you get from smoking three packs a day and then spending all night howling at the moon.

Surprised, I looked over at him. He hadn't moved, but I

was sure he had spoken. "Come again?"

"He threw it away." His voice was raw as he pointed to the radio. "Clifford."

"Threw what away?" I asked.

"His gift. He didn't want it anymore."

I tapped my mug on the counter and Rosie came over to refill it. "What are you talkin' about, Pops?" I asked as Rosie swayed over. Ah, she was something.

The old man waited until Rosie had left before answering. He coughed into a dirty 'kerchief, reached into his pocket and pulled out a cigarette case. Putting a cigarette in his mouth, he lit a match and inhaled deeply. "You think these great artists come by their talent naturally?"

"Sure. Why not?"

"They don't," he grumbled. "It's given to them."

I shrugged, decided he was screwy, and dug in to my slice of cherry pie.

Three bites in, I could tell the old man was staring at me. I put my fork down, turned to face him. The whites of his eyes were the color of faded wallpaper. "Look, I don't know what you're talkin' about, but I'd like to just enjoy my pie and coffee, huh?"

He smiled, yellow teeth as big as a horse's. "You're what, thirty, John?"

I damn near fell out of my chair. "How do you know my name?"

"I know a lot, John," He held out his hand. "I'm Buddy." I took his dry, cracked hand in mine, gave it a pump. "Let's go outside and talk." He dropped two bits on the counter, stood and walked out the door.

I chuckled, nervously, I admit, and scooped another bite of pie. No way in hell I was following him.

The fork stopped halfway to my mouth. He knew my name. How? I was nobody that anybody knew by looking at me. I turned, looking out the window. He stood on the street corner watching the traffic, waiting.

I turned back to the counter, looked at the pie, at Rosie, at Marge, then back out the window. He hadn't moved.

Curiosity, if nothing else, made me move.

I dropped a dollar on the counter, put on my hat and walked out. I lit a smoke and stood next to him on the corner. He grinned and said, "Walk with me, John."

We turned up the street and were silent for most of a block. It was a nice June morning, a promise hanging in the air.

"You can feel it, can't you?" He looked sideways at me. "Something big is about to happen."

I shrugged, stomped on the cigarette butt.

"Talent," his voice took on a tone of importance, "is given. It's borrowed, loaned out. It always has to be returned."

"That so?"

"Yes," he coughed. "Clifford decided he was done with it. I collected and now I'm going to loan it out again."

"Man, you are crazy," I stopped to confront him. "I admit you almost had me by dropping my name. But, you could have figured that out from someone. Most everyone in the diner knows me. Now this garbage about loaning out talent. What are you? Some crossroads devil come to tempt me like Robert Johnson was?"

He chuckled. "No, I just work for him. Think of me as a middle man."

"You're cracked." I hurried my steps and turned down an alley that was a shortcut back to my apartment.

At the end of the alley, he was waiting for me.

"How did you…" I pointed at him then back down the alley from which I came.

"I've been trying to tell you, John. I'm making you an offer. This is very real."

"Wha…" I shook my head. "Why me?"

"Why you?" He smiled. "You are on the cusp to greatness, but on your current path, you will not make it. I'm here to make it happen."

"Greatness, you say?" He had me now, but not entirely. "So, this is a crossroads deal? You come for my soul in three years? That it?"

"Not so harsh as that," he smiled. "You keep it for as long as you like. If you want to give it up early, you can. You want to keep it until you grow old and die, you can." He shrugged. "But the end result will always be the same."

"And what's that?"

He fixed me with his rheumy stare. "You die and your soul goes below. Immediately."

"What happened to Brownie?"

"Clifford grew afraid and began to hate the fame. It happens sometimes. He made the choice to do away with it. I was sent to take it and him."

"And now you want to give it to me? And I can keep it until my end days?" I was starting to warm up to this idea. "Seems like you get the short end, huh?"

"Maybe," he smiled evilly then. "Except for the eternal suffering, John."

I looked at him hard and gave him my answer.

The following year, 1957, I released my debut album.

I called it *Coltrane*.

∞

Tumblin' Dice

His house retreated in the rear-view, family snuggly asleep inside. Everything he would need to start over was in the trunk, the back seat. The Strat rode shotgun, its sunburst body vibrant.

Sunlight glared in his eyes as he knuckled the stereo on. Jagger and Richards were rolling the dice, sixes, sevens and nines. He tapped his finger in time, singing along, seeing the chords on his inner fret board: car jamming.

For so long he had lived for others, his insides were hollow. He was taking the gig in the city. The dice stopped tumbling and he was free.

☙❧

Shinji and the Yorei

The Pearl of the Tides glowed softly in the misty light of the *Asaguroi Mizu*, the Dark Water. Shinji held it out before him, letting the light guide his way. So far, it was a sound idea. The Pearl had guided him along the hidden path through the bog. His sandals dangled from a string around his neck and clunked together every third step. He wore knee-length trousers, a loose fitting shirt and the wide, cone-shaped straw hat common among peasants. A thin bamboo staff helped steady his way over the grass hummocks that dotted the path.

It was said that in the center of the bog lived Sagura Yumi, a wise woman of great skill. Others said that Yumi was a witch. Whatever you believed, no one knew for sure because the *Asaguroi Mizu* was too treacherous to travel.

Shinji had solved that problem by finding the Pearl of the Tides. The Pearl would reveal any path the holder wished for. Shinji had gone to great lengths to get it; selling all he owned and spending the entire family fortune to find it. Now, he traveled as any other peasant, with nothing but the shirt on his back.

The Pearl guided him true. After only a few more minutes along the path, he saw a light in the distance. As he approached, a small cottage came into view. What else could it be in this ancestor forsaken bog but the house of Sagura Yumi? Shinji quickened his pace. After all the years of seeking, he would finally find what he sought.

An ancient woman stepped through the door of the cottage. She was short and gaunt, her bones showing more than her flesh. Her kimono was threadbare and hanging from her shoulders, as was a shamisen that had seen better days.

She shuffled over to a small bench, sat down and placed the shamisen in her lap. She grasped a bachi and set about tuning the instrument.

When Shinji approached, the old woman looked up and smiled a toothless grin. "Ah! It is not often I have an audience for my daily practice." Shinji listened as she began to play a long forgotten gagaku from the courts of Kyoto.

"You play well," Shinji complimented. "I do not recognize the tune."

"It is old," the woman said as she continued to play. "Older even than me!" She barked a laugh.

Shinji smiled and waited until the song was done. He sketched a small bow, a mere politeness. "Are you Sagura Yumi?"

"Ahh," she breathed. "Sagura Yumi has been dead many years."

"Oh," Shinji frowned. "I had thought that perhaps you were she." He gestured to the cottage. "I did not think any one else lived out here."

"This was Yumi's house," the old woman said as she set the shamisen down. "Why do you seek her?"

Shinji squatted, laid the staff across his knees and

pushed the hat back off his head so that it hung down his back. "My wife. She was the one thing I loved more than anything in this world. She took ill two summers ago and passed. I have been searching for a way to be with her again—to bring her back—all that time."

"Ohh! Is that so?" the old woman looked shocked. "Why would you? She has passed on to the spirits and so to her ancestors. Why would you look to take her away from that?"

"I am empty inside without her," Shinji's eyes never left his lap. "I sold all that I owned and spent all the money I had in order to find Sagura Yumi. Now, to hear she is dead, I am lost for true."

"You were foolish, it seems to me," the old woman tapped a finger against her cheek. "Perhaps there is something I can do."

"You? What can you do?" Shinji's skepticism curled his lips. "You are nothing but an old woman."

"Perhaps," she agreed. "But that gem you carry." She pointed to the pouch on Shinji's belt. "It is the Pearl of the Tides, is it not? I know its secrets and can use it to help you."

"You can?" Shinji jumped up, tugging at the pouch, all skepticism vanished. "What do I need to do?" he asked.

"Merely give me the Pearl. I will do the rest," the old woman licked her lips and held out her hand.

Shinji placed the Pearl in her outstretched hand and took a step back. The old woman closed her fingers around the gem and smiled. "Fool!" she spat at Shinji.

"What?" Shinji gasped as the old woman and the cottage seemed to grow taller. A glow surrounded her and she stood straight and tall.

"Now, be with your wife," the woman said. Shinji

looked down and saw that the woman and cottage were not getting bigger, he was sinking into the bog. He struggled, throwing himself one way and then the next, tried to climb out, but he only sank further. He tried grabbing the old woman, but she stepped back casually and laughed. Looking around for something to grab, Shinji saw a thick tree root sticking from the mire. He grabbed and pulled. He began to rise, but the stick suddenly came free with a sickening *slurp.* Now holding it, Shinji saw that the stick was not a tree root, but a bone. From the size, he knew it to be a human leg bone.

He threw the bone at the old woman, but she waved her hand and the bone flew away into a bush. Shinji now saw that littered all around the cottage, bones of all types protruded from the bog. He screamed in horror.

"Yes, now you see," the old woman laughed. "You will join your wife with the spirits. That is what you wanted? To be with your wife?"

"No!" Shinji howled. "Not like this!"

The old woman *tsked.* "But it is so much easier this way. Bringing back the dead is messy." Shinji had sunk up to his chest and had stopped struggling, but was uttering a constant string of curses at the old woman. She shrugged her shoulders and held up the Pearl. "I suppose I should have done more for you because of this beauty," the Pearl flashed, "but, no witnesses means no wagging tongues, eh?"

Shinji was up to his neck and crying silently.

"The power of the Pearl will restore me once again to being Sagura Yumi and I will be yorei no longer!"

The bog swallowed Shinji as the ghost of Sagura Yumi capered in delight.

ଔଌ

The Fine Print

"You're five hundred ten gil short, Kablah."

"Am I?" the rakshasa asked, raising a striped eyebrow. "I was certain your share was only fifteen hundred."

The vrock's eye ridges came together in a show of concentration as he counted the coins again. "Fifteen hundred. That's five hundred ten short. I should have gotten two thousand forty-two. One-third of the total gain."

Kablah looked over the papers he had scattered before him on the table. Choosing one, he shook some ale drops from it and held it up to the light. "Yes, your contract states that you should receive one-third of the gains, providing that you fulfill the terms."

"Terms! No one had mentioned terms!" The vrock swung its vulture-like head towards the third being seated at the table. "Did you know about terms, Valfor?"

The bat-winged teifling slowly raised his eyes from the book he was reading. "Of course. Didn't you read the contract, Baatezu? If memory serves, and it always does, the contract states that an individual's gains will be reduced by one-quarter should any outside help be used by said individual and that one quarter should be distributed evenly between the remaining party members," Valfor looked to Kablah for confirmation, and he nodded in agreement. "Baatezu, summoning five dregs from the abyss to help us slay those adventurers constitutes a breach in contract and results in Kablah and myself splitting that five-hundred-ten gil."

"He's right, Baatezu. It's all here in the contract," Kablah waved the paper in front of the demon's beak.

The vrock stood from his chair and flapped his wings agitatedly, setting loose a small flurry of gray feathers that floated gently to the floor.

"Argh! You try and cheat me! We would never have been able to beat them without the dregs! That mage was very powerful and the small one was too fast to catch!"

"Yes, the mage was powerful, the rogue was fast, the fighter was strong and the priest kept reigning holy might upon my head," Kablah growled. "But we were to beat them unaided. It was a test set forth by our employer, Baatezu. A test which you failed."

"He is right, vrock," Valfor said from behind his book. "And as such, I believe our employer will not be requiring your services anymore." Valfor stood from the table, closing his book. "Kablah and I go to meet him now. I suggest you stay here with what gil you have and seek other employment. Come, Kablah." The teifling stuffed his book into his pack and left the tavern with the rakshasa close behind.

Baatezu sat alone at the table, confused about what had just happened. He was now unemployed with less money than he thought he would have. As he was scraping the coins into his money bag, he overheard a conversation at the table next to him.

Leaning over to the minotaur at the next table, Baatezu

asked, "I hear you need a fourth member for your group. I am seeking employment."

The minotaur looked the vrock up and down and grunted. "You look tough enough. Here's the group contract." He handed Baatezu a piece of parchment.

Without even looking at the text, Baatezu asked, "Have you got a quill?"

ଔ

Bastogne
The Ardennes Trilogy, Part 1

It wasn't what I was expecting.

For two years, all you heard or saw was how glorious it was. The newsreels showed gruff men smiling, holding the spoils of war. Tanks hurled across the desert, firing their big guns. The fleets of ships and planes—all of it—got me to enlist the day I turned eighteen.

Ma cried that day. I wouldn't be surprised if she still is. Pa... well, Pa just shook my hand and said, "Good luck." Turned his back to it all.

I left them, still a boy, head filled with the glories of war.

It was December 2, 1944 when I arrived at Camp Mourmelon, outside the village of *Mour-melon-le-Grand*, France. I was assigned to C Company, 506th Regiment, 101st Airborne. These men I had to be a part of were frightening. They strutted around the camp, fully outfitted with live ammunition, hand grenades, and unauthorized firearms. They smelled bad, were unshaven and never smiled. These were not the heroes from the newsreels. These were murderers.

Two days after my arrival, the temperature dropped to

below freezing. Being in camp behind the lines, it wasn't too bad. We had heat, showers and hot food, but that morning, all of my extra clothes were missing. When I brought the theft up to my sergeant, he scoffed and said I wouldn't last long enough to need any of it. He really didn't care. None of them did. We new recruits meant nothing to them.

We weren't with them for Normandy, Carentan, Hell's Highway or the Island. We were green, untested and not their brothers. We were the shunned, the ones they knew would die first.

And so, they made no effort to get to know us. We... I, was alone.

On December 19, we marched for Bastogne. As part of the 101st, we were set up on the line as part of a giant ring defense. The devastation in that area was like nothing I had ever seen. As we were marching in, the men we were relieving were marching out. They were defeated, starved, wounded and frost-bitten. They were the walking dead and we were about to take their place.

I will never forget that first shelling. It was at night and I was freezing in a foxhole, praying that my feet were okay because they didn't hurt anymore. The noise was unbearable. Explosions were everywhere and the screams of wounded and dying men is a sound that will haunt me from this world into the next. So many explosions, it was like the sun had risen.

We were supposed to fight back. Get up and fire our rifles. Not many of us could.

All I could think of was that somewhere back home, my mother was still crying.

Eventually, the shelling stopped. I had no idea how much time had passed, but the real sun was halfway to noon. I was in one piece. Many of the others were not.

I was ordered out of my hole to help with the wounded. It was gruesome work. The medics were frantic, helping those they could while we bore stretchers to carry away the men who would get shipped back to Bastogne proper where a hospital was set up. Hopefully, some of those men would be sent home.

One of the last men I helped that day—I never knew his name—said to me as I loaded him onto the truck, "Hey kid, don't worry. They got us surrounded, the poor bastards."

With those words, I finally understood what it meant to be a part of the 101st Airborne. True, I was green and probably would end up on a stretcher myself, if not shipped home in a box, but those words gave me hope. Being a part of the brotherhood with these men wasn't about looking and acting tough, it was an attitude of toughness borne from living through experiences that should have killed you.

It wasn't what I was expecting.

ଔଓ

Journal Entry: November 18, 2012

Football Sunday. Three hours until the Pats game, watching the Jets and hoping for a loss. Computer tied up due to conducting an info-dump to an external HDD.

Started reading *Camp Concentration* yesterday and its journal format reminded me of this notebook. Grand ideas of writing in it everyday. We shall see.

I've been feeling out of sorts lately. Mostly a lack of concentration. I hope that daily handwriting will help increase focus.

A number of projects are on the table at this time: writing prompts to keep my imagination in practice, Easy Money, Mr. Lux, Hannah Anne, a superhero story for D. I think the workload is affecting my mood.

ന്ദ

Too Tired

He came home late from work again. The light was on in the kitchen, but she was nowhere to be seen. He dropped his coat and briefcase in the den, anxious for some sleep. When he reached the stairs, there were two sets of clothes scattered leading up the steps; hers and a man's. Not his. The pictures leading up the wall were askew; one had fallen and rested on the first step, face down.

He paused, one foot on the first step, white-knuckled hand on the banister. Soft murmuring drifted down from the bedroom. He bent and picked up the frame, turning it over. His face and hers smiled back at him, white sand, palm trees and a sapphire ocean behind. Sighing, he dropped the picture on the carpeted steps and turned around, trudging to the kitchen and retrieving a beer from the refrigerator.

Flopping onto the couch, he twisted the cap off the bottle and turned on the television.

Someday he was going to say something, but tonight he was just too tired.

ଓଃ

Cracks

Dim light filters under the door from the light in the hall. It's an old bulb, hanging from the ceiling by a fraying wire. Sometimes it swings, sending shadows chasing each other around the room.

My eyes seek the light like a moth, room tilted in a worm's view from where I lay on the tattered mattress. It smells of urine and mildew. A rusted spring digs into my hip where it has torn the skin, a coppery-brown spot marking the place. One jagged toenail snags on the fringe. I flex and the nail slowly pulls free from my toe in a wash of pain. Mouth too dry to even moan, I remain silent.

Yesterday, or this morning (it's impossible to judge time in this place), a tooth fell out. Weakly, I tried to spit it to the floor, but only just pushed it out with my swollen tongue. It's cavernous rot sits by my nose.

I think that I may be dying.

This Purgatorian room has been marked by time. Once sterile green walls are now faded with disease, cracked and peeling. In a few places, the floor tiles are gone, others loose. There are brown stains on the walls.

There is something on the other side, waiting, watching. I can hear it in the shadows, a constant susurration of promises and demands seeping through the cracks. Always in the shadows, the whispers chase one another, avoiding the light.

When the light swings, the cracks in the wall stare back. Ethereal eyes watching from beyond, their gaze a wool blanket making my skin crawl.

The light is all that keeps it on the other side. Its strength is in the shadows. I can feel it reaching, grasping from the cracks in the darkness. When the light swings, the susurration angers, recedes. It promises death then. Rending and blood.

Yesterday, or perhaps this evening, or even a week ago, the light went out.

ঔ

Stadtnacht

I look at the street through an orange haze. Color has lost all meaning. Green has become a black illness and the sidewalk glows like a dying ember. A car goes by—loudly—the branches of low shrubs dancing in its wake. The air feels stale and thick, breath comes heavily.

The windows of the houses I walk by throw useless light into the dark. Others are black as pitch. I wonder what lives are lived behind those portals. Mundane, boring, the everyday sort? Are they nine to five lives, supper at six, sex on Fridays? I imagine lives. There, a thief. That one, a wife beater. The owner of the sports car? Cheating on his wife while she spends every Wednesday afternoon with her lover in leathery passion. The house with the peeling paint—a crack dealer. The worlds I have created for these people. Would they appreciate them?

The sidewalk roils and tumbles under my gait. Piles, discarded by lives, lay on the edge spilling into the street. The bittersweet assails my nose. I breathe deeply and pause. Apples and…something else…?

Stale wine.

I woke this morning not knowing whether I would remember my name. I felt a vague unease as I stumbled into the bathroom, my bladder bursting, until my reflection whispered it to me. Every morning my reflection makes me a reality. Every morning I get the affirmation I need to walk out the door.

Now, I stand here amid the smell of apples and bad wine, looking at this city through the hellish light and I wonder. Who walks by my house and makes up my life?

Another car flashes by, a dozen pieces of paper swirling in mad eddies behind it. I follow the trail of paper, the sidewalk moves again. At the very edge of vision, a movement. I stop and turn.

In the window is a woman, her rust-colored hair metallic in the artificial light. She's holding a phone to her ear, laughing, her free hand moving in circles to the rhythm of her mouth. I watch her, thinking, Will she undress? Instantly, the thought leaves to be replaced by another.

Who is she talking to?

Her mother? Boyfriend?

I look at her a moment longer before deciding that the energy to give her a life is not there. It is much easier to do so for the faceless.

The concrete tumbles on again under my feet. A sharp silvery light pierces my eye. Through a break in the gray blanket, she gazes down, dispelling the burning light. I look at her, admiring her duo-tone face.

I walk on, not knowing where. The city passes me by in a soft blur of dulled colors.

Later, I sit outside the house of God, my ears assailed now by the dull roar of the urban landscape. I peer through the nighttime orange haze—watching. How many lives? This city seems an infinite store of humanity; their sounds cut out as they hurry by, the breath of the urban beast drowning them out.

Through the open door come the faint strains of the choir deeply involved in practice.

The sky is striped with night and silver. I am too weak to write much more. But I can still hear them walking in the streets; not speaking. The precise mathematics of an ancient *kapellmeister* carries me up and out of urbanity, and I soar.

ଔ

Ghost in the Machine

He pulled into the drive, headlights showing the rotted wood of the garage door in the midnight darkness. *I still need to fix that*, he thought, then smiled crookedly. He shook his head and let out a soft *phffft* of breath. No, it wouldn't ever get fixed.

The ignition clicked off and he sighed in dread. What he was about to do had to be done.

He got out of the car and closed the door quietly. Gingerly walking over the uneven driveway in the dark, his toe found the broken concrete step of the front walkway. Habit forced him to walk to the left side of the slab, dodging phantom shrubs he had torn out of the ground a month before. As usual, she had not left the porch light on, so he was forced to walk carefully, judging in the darkness the location of the porch steps. There was no moon that night; only the light from the neighbor's house across the street glinting off of the pseudo-brass doorknob gave him any way-point for his short journey. Like a sailor of old guided by the North Star, he latched onto the brassy glint until he stood before the solid oak door.

Standing there while he fingered his keys, he could still faintly smell the stain he had used on the door to give it that dark color she had wanted. That door stood out from the rest of the run-down house like a homeless man wearing a brand new pair of shoes. It just didn't look as if it belonged there. Fumbling the key into the lock, the door opened on silent hinges.

The house was dark and smelled faintly of the litter box. The cats would be sleeping with her in the bed as usual, which meant he would be sleeping on the couch. But not tonight. He closed the door, first turning the doorknob lock, then the deadbolt.

With a calm that did not betray the butterflies in his stomach, he put his keys back into his pocket instead of putting them on the small table by the door. The sudden urge to urinate was surprising. As he walked by the mirror his father had made for him as a house-gift, he looked into the refection, eyes having already adjusted to the weak light filtering in from outside and did not recognize the face of grim determination that stared back at him.

Wincing with every creak of the floor, his footsteps took him to the bathroom. Only after closing the door did he turn on the light. The bathroom was a mess as usual and it stank. Not for the first time did he wonder what she had done all day. Wet towels littered the floor and the tiles were starting to come loose from their adhesive around the toilet. He lifted the toilet seat and quickly turned his head. It hadn't been flushed all day, it seemed. Swallowing the sudden rise of bile, he relieved himself.

Back in the hall, the lights out, he walked to their bedroom. Steps taken by habit, he could navigate his house without the light. He stood in the doorway, facing towards the bed, trying to will her shape under the blankets to vision. She would be on the left side, curled in a fetal position; the two cats sprawled out next to her on the right side. He needed no light, no visual cues to do what had to be done.

DO WHAT MUST BE DONE, it had told him. He reached into his back pocket and withdrew the razor-sharp scalpel he found in the Dumpster last week at the hospital. *She has to go. I have to get on with my life. I deserve better than this.*

He took a step into the room, all his attention focused on the invisible bed, her invisible form. Another step. A third. The floorboard creaked, loudly. His breath hissed and his face contorted in rage. She stirred, moaning softly in her sleep. "Rick…" she breathed happily. Not his name.

His face fell. Fingers loosened their grip on the scalpel. *No. Not tonight. This is wrong.* Just as silently as he entered, he backed out of the bedroom, closed the door and put the scalpel in his shirt pocket.

His study was at the other end of their modest home, over the garage, five steps up from the living room. Once again, he made his way in the dark, without sight or sonar. He climbed the steps, habit allowing him to avoid the one protruding nail on the third step, and opened the door when he reached the top. Entering, he closed the door and flicked the light switch.

She had been in this room today, using his net-gear. The neural plug was thrown carelessly to the floor, its tip resting in some type of fluid she had spilled onto the carpet, probably beer, instead of soaking in the jar of disinfectant. She still couldn't grasp the concept that the plug had to remain clean in order to prevent a direct infection of the brain. With a snarl, he yanked the cord from the floor and thrust it into the disinfectant.

He flipped on the CPU and the wall screen burst to life with the day's latest headlines. Ignoring the growing trouble among the lunar colonists, he adjusted the suspensor chair, preparing for a foray into the net's seedier side.

Pulling the neural plug from the jar, he jammed the 'gear into the socket at the base of his skull and fell into the suspensor chair. Neural linked to the net, he keyed in the address for a Bulgarian skin flick. It was one of many such serial pornography flicks found on the net, easily accessible and free to all. Pornography was still illegal in the North American Alliance, but many of the countries in Eurasia had passed laws making certain types of skin flicks legal. The ICE he had bought to bypass the NAA's security protocols against porn had cost him a month's pay, but as far as he was concerned, the Bulgarian serials were worth it.

The wall screen flickered and he was shown a choice of various episodes running back two weeks. There were also two new installments that he hadn't seen yet. He punched up the first one.

Adda Schultz, a German native, was the star of this episode. She was also his favorite. He watched with a feeling akin to love; not real love, the neural connection stimulated basic emotions in the brain, putting the viewer as much into the flick as possible. He had an erection within seconds and had no difficulty imagining the lithe Adda on top of him as he climaxed. Much better than the lump of uselessness that was currently asleep in his bed, he thought.

As he lay there panting with Adda still on the screen, her insatiability nearly killing the actor who was playing a farmhand, the voice came to him again. He could never distinguish exact words but he could understand what the voice was conveying to him. *YOU ARE BETTER THAN THIS. YOU DESERVE MORE. SHE'S HOLDING YOU BACK. GET RID OF HER.* Over and over. It was what had prompted him earlier this evening to use the scalpel on his wife. *WHY DIDN'T YOU GO THROUGH WITH IT? YOU WERE SO CLOSE TO FREEDOM.* I couldn't. I hate her but it's wrong. *IT'S THE ONLY WAY.* No, there has to be another way. *YOU KNOW THERE ISN'T. DO WHAT NEEDS TO BE DONE.* Then it was gone.

Every night the voice had come to him for the past half a year. At first he was able to ignore it. He was able to pass it off as his own mind playing tricks on him due to stress. But the voice was always there, every night, urging him to do the unthinkable. Tonight, he had almost given in to it. He had hoped that the voice would stop if only he did kill his wife. He knew it was wrong and had not been able to.

Now the voice seemed to know that he had tried and failed. Until tonight, the voice had been like a skipping phonograph, the same message over and over. Tonight, he realized that it knew; that it was aware of what he was doing even when not jacked in.

Visual flashes came next, as they always did. She was torn to pieces, she was cut up, she was strangled. Hundreds of grisly deaths clicked in his mind's eye as fast as you could click a camera shutter. Sweat beaded on his brow and his lips pulled back in a grim rictus. His body shook with tremors, the suspensor chair gently rocking. As suddenly as they came, the visions stopped.

He was in the living room, mid-stride, his head just having been jerked back. Looking behind him, he saw the neural plug and cord lying on the floor where it had pulled from his socket when it reached its full length. He didn't remember leaving the study. He didn't remember taking the scalpel out of his pocket.

He loomed over her in the dark, the scalpel poised over her throat. Both cats stared at him with green-eyed indifference. *Wasn't I just in the living room?* He lowered the scalpel in confusion.

Sunlight gently caressed his face and he breathed deeply, waking from a restful sleep. He began to smile, but a cold stickiness ran along his back. Turning over, he screamed at the bloody gash in her neck. Her dead eyes threw accusation at him. He leapt from the bed, covered in sticky, half-dry blood. The cats were cut too, the scalpel still stuck in the eye of the calico. He fell to his knees, screaming.

Across the house in the study, the vid screen flickered to life, one giant eye gazing out in satisfaction.

ઙ઼ଓ

Red Rover
The Ardennes Trilogy, Part 2

The shelling had gone on for days. The Krauts would take a few hours off each night, but when the sun rose, we all heard the *whump! whump!* of the 88's coming to life again. Seconds later, noise and fire erupted all around us and wouldn't stop until well past sun-down.

We lost a lot of good guys in Bastogne. Jimmy, Mac, Sal, Johnny—too many, too soon. We lost a lot of the new guys too—Greens just out of boot who thought Normandy was a legend, and I suppose to them it was. We were the tough guys, the veterans. The Greens looked up to us, but we avoided them. We had learned what it was like to lose a buddy and we didn't want any more buddies.

If the shells and the bullets didn't get you, the cold did. That's what happened to Lieutenant Walker. He started a cough, worse than the rest of us, but it was when his feet turned black from frostbite that the medics shipped him back to Mourmelon. A Green was promoted to take his place—Lieutenant Jones. Jones looked to me like a school teacher, all thin, pointy nose and glasses. He never said much, just let us vets do what we did. Which was fine with us. We didn't need an inexperienced officer who would probably run at the first sign of real trouble telling us what to do.

When the sun rose on the 23rd, we didn't hear the 88's start up. It was quiet. Looking out over the grazing field toward Foy, it was all fog and silence. We were uneasy.

Lt. Jones dropped into my foxhole, a question on his face.

"I don't know, sir," I whispered to him. "Might be they ran out of ammo?"

"Not likely," the Lieutenant whispered back. "They've got a solid supply line into Foy."

The silence continued for an hour. We were on edge, expecting an all-out attack at any second.

What we got was a voice.

One of the Krauts, probably an officer, was shouting to us across the pasture. I didn't know what he was saying, but he kept repeating the same thing.

"We have anyone who speaks German?" Jones asked.

"Yessir," I pointed east. "Schwartz does."

"Go get him."

Just as I was about to climb out of the foxhole, Schwartz jumped in.

"Lieutenant, the Germans are asking for our surrender," he said between gulps of air.

"Our surrender?"

"Yessir," Schwartz wiped his mouth. "They say that if we approach slowly across the pasture, hands up, they will accept our defeat."

Jones looked at Schwartz a moment before he began laughing. I couldn't help thinking for a moment that this soft Green officer was just happy to get out of a foxhole.

"Sir?" I asked.

Jones's laughter subsided to chuckles. "I was just reminded of Jeanette Soltz, Sergeant."

"Sir?" I asked again.

"Jeanette used to be the caller when we played Red Rover when I was a kid," he chuckled. "Little cheater, she was."

Schwartz and I shared a look, wondering if Jones had lost it.

"What are we going to do, sir?" Schwartz asked.

Jones stopped chuckling and gave us a level stare. "I never trusted Jeanette Soltz." The Lieutenant grinned. "Tell the boys to dig in. We ain't going anywhere."

☙❧

Journal Entry: November 23, 2012

Sitting at the desk today sans laptop. An odd feeling writing this way. It brings back memories of childhood homework.

Camp Concentration has been a humbling experience. The vocabulary and references confuse me and I don't understand much of it. I can't help but think that if I had stuck to college it would be easier. I won't ever be able to write at that level, I know, but it bothers me that I can't.

I can't remember why it's been four days since my last entry. Perhaps the kids' vacation is the reason?

Just distracted by the noise of a loud truck. For such a secluded spot, our road sees a lot of truck traffic.

Lately, blog readership and interaction has declined. I reserve judgment until next week.

"Can't Fool the Blues" has lost my interest and D. has grown frustrated with my lack of production, I'm sure. I constantly post that I am working on the Hannah Anne book, but I have not even started yet. Something is holding me back and I can always find an excuse to not work on it.

Am I really a writer? Or just a sham?

I didn't sleep well last night—dreams of monstrous alligators devouring me.

I don't like reading a book that makes me feel stupid.

ɞ

Wolfmother

The wolfmother's eyes rage hellfire into my soul. My annual trip finds me here, year after year, staring at Romulus and Remus, brushed by *de la Fosse*. The scene runs floor to ceiling and wall to wall, much too big for my tastes.

Whoever furnished the room placed no furniture along that wall, you can see every brush stroke. The bed is on the opposite wall, and, late at night, the red neon from the No Vacancy sign glows within the wolfmother's eyes. She watches me watching her. She watches me when I sleep.

I find no comfort in it. There is no protection here.

One year, I asked to be moved to a different room, but they were booked, they said, it couldn't be done. The conference and all, you see? I reluctantly acknowledged that I did see. Perhaps next year I can be placed in a room with a different mural? Oh, none of the rooms have a mural. We painted all the walls eggshell.

But every year the wolfmother stares, the founders of that once great ancient empire suckle, and I dream the stories that have become my life and my fame.

My curse.

Each night for seven days, she comes to me, crimson eyes glowing and whispers in my sleeping ears. Seven stories. Tell them true, she says, honor the agreement.

And I do. I must.

The first year, seventeen years ago, I ignored her. I thought it was a dream. Her stories went untold.

Seven people died. Friends, colleagues, family.

My daughter.

All accidents. Seven deaths for seven untold stories.

The second year, I had no choice but to attend the conference. I was given the same room. It was when I asked to be moved. No, it wasn't ever going to be that simple.

We confronted each other in my dream-scape that first night. Argued and fought. Eventually she showed me the ancient contract. I had to tell her stories as agreed centuries ago by a long forgotten ancestor. I had no choice.

She told me to listen carefully and then spun her tale. The next day I stayed in the room, sat on the floor facing her, and scratched out her story in my little notebook. I held it to her face, angry, asked if it was right. Did I leave anything out? I seethed. Is this your story? I raged. Is this what you want from me?

She didn't answer and I despaired.

So it has been, year after year, I tell her stories.

People know my name.

I have been on television.

I have three houses, a new wife and family, movie deals and books being translated into fifty different languages.

I am a slave to her words.

This year, I have listened to her stories. I have written them down. I have left the room and returned home.

Desperation drove me to burning the notebook and

beginning my own story. A story about lupine eyes bleeding hellfire.

My wife died. The funeral was nice. The people were nice. My son and daughter cried. I did not.

I wrote about stories told in dreams. Stories of horror, death and insanity. True stories.

My son died. The funeral was nice. The people were nice. My daughter cried. I have become hollow inside.

I wrote about the ancient contract. I wrote about the price of stories untold.

My daughter died. The funeral was nice. The people were nice. The police were not. Too many have died they said. Yes, I agreed, far too many.

My publisher fell in love with my story. Best ever, she told me. I smiled wanly. It is my last one, I told her in a whisper. A true one. Someone, somewhere, needs to believe that.

Only then will I be free of the wolfmother.

ଓଃଽ୬

The Charles River Baptism

It had been ten years of pain and blame. Ten years of self-doubt, depression, prescription drugs and alcohol. Ten years of being afraid, of being alone, of not being able to look at the opposite sex. Ten years of a string of therapists who could not help.

Ellie sat in the passenger seat, knuckles white from clutching her knees, bathed in the morning sun. Deborah said something, but Ellie's head was floating in a haze of fear. Body moving stiff-legged, she opened the door, climbed out, and walked.

Fifty yards from the car, Ellie stopped.

"It was here," she heard herself say.

"Are you sure?" Deborah touched Ellie's arm and then withdrew it when Ellie flinched. "This is such a peaceful place," said the therapist. "Let's sit on the bench."

The lone bench, its green paint chipped at the corners, glistened with dew. Deborah made a face and began searching in her bag. The Charles River flowed past quietly this early in the morning and the city on the far bank was a shadowy mass in the dawn. There was no fence here to keep pedestrians from the water. A Harvard crew glided past them, oars scooping the water.

Paralyzed with memory, Ellie didn't move, didn't see the world in front of her. She saw the city's night-time glow on the water, felt a chill in the air, a need to be alone, and a growing feeling of purpose being dashed by rough hands throwing her down, breath like rotten onions, a forcing of her legs apart…

"Ellie!" Deborah's startled shout broke Ellie from her reverie. She was on her knees, tears streaming down her face, breath coming in ragged gasps.

Deborah knelt beside her. "When I said you needed to confront your fears, I meant in the safety of my office. Let's go back."

Ellie choked on sobs. "No, it's time."

"Ellie," Deborah helped her stand, "I really think this is a bad idea."

Ellie brushed hair from her face and wiped her eyes. "You're new to me, Deborah. You don't know everything yet. It's time for me."

"Okay," Deborah said. "Why don't we sit down on the bench and you can tell me, all right?" She produced a wad of tissues from her bag and wiped the dew from the bench as best she could. Ellie sat, crossing her legs. Deborah followed.

Both women looked out over the river for a few minutes. When Deborah looked to Ellie, it was clear the woman was gathering her thoughts.

"When I was a little girl," Ellie began, "my father used to take me fishing. We lived in upstate New York, not the Catskills that the City calls upstate, but I mean north of Albany in the Adirondack foothills."

She paused, flinching when Deborah laid an

encouraging hand on her leg.

"Don't," Ellie pulled her leg away. "I don't like being touched."

"I'm sorry," Deborah placed her hands in her lap. "I'm only trying to show you I care and I'm listening."

"That's what I'm paying you for, isn't it?" Ellie asked. "But you don't. Not really."

Deborah said nothing. The quiet stretched.

"Anyway," Ellie continued, not looking at Deborah, "he used to take me through the woods to a brook nearby the house and we'd fish for trout. In those days, it was woods and farms everywhere, only small neighborhoods of houses. We could see deer and turkeys in our backyard in the spring and summer. It was a nice place.

"He used to tell me stories while we fished. Ones he made up, I guess, I'm not sure. One year, a beaver family dammed the brook and built a lodge. He made up stories about them, very *Wind in the Willows* stuff. He used to tell me that the fish were water spirits, or lost mermaids, or nixies; it was always something different. So, we always threw the fish back. He said it would bring us luck."

"Did it?" Deborah asked.

Ellie shook her head. "No. I visited my parents a few years ago. Our woods were gone, replaced by houses and big stores, streets and lights. The brook was gone too, all dried up," Ellie sighed. "Dad died a few weeks later from colon cancer. He was only fifty-six. So no, I don't think it brought him any luck."

"What about you?"

"Me?" Ellie asked. "No. Not me either."

"You don't think so?" Deborah dug through her bag, removed a lighter and a beat up pack of Marlboro's. "Do you mind?"

Ellie shook her head. "No, go ahead."

Deborah lit a cigarette, blew out a cloud of blue smoke. "Why didn't the fish bring you luck?"

Ellie crossed her arms, hugging herself. "After high school," her voice was quiet and drifted in wisps among the cigarette smoke, "I went to college." She closed her eyes, turning her face to the sun. "I wanted to be a writer, or an English teacher, but college didn't agree with me. I dropped out after a few months."

Deborah exhaled blue smoke once more then crushed out her cigarette. "That's too bad. Did you ever go back? Do you blame the fish?"

"No," Ellie rubbed her hands on her thighs. "I moved here. I figured I could get a job writing or find some entry-level position at a publishing house." She shrugged. "Without a degree, it was no use. I worked through a temp agency for creative types, mostly jobs proofreading or writing blurbs for websites. I tried publishing some short stories in magazines, but it was always, 'It's not what we're looking for right now.' Rejection after rejection."

"You see yourself as a failure," Deborah said.

Ellie crossed her arms again. "Yes, I do. Wouldn't you?"

"I don't know," Deborah answered. "We're not the same person." She sighed. "What about friends? Didn't you have anyone to talk to?"

Ellie nodded. "Relationships too. I could never stay in one more than a few months. Always there was something wrong with him." She paused, then whispered, "Or me."

Deborah glanced at her watch. "Is that why you were here that night ten years ago?"

"Yes," Ellie said. "The river calmed me, helped me

think. The sound of it, the smell of it; it reminded me of home and fishing with my dad." She squeezed herself tight. "That was taken from me. This is the first time I've been here since that night. I never felt like I belonged here in Boston; that the whole move was a big mistake. I always felt trapped here." She looked at the river, longing in her eyes. "The river was my slice of home and then it was taken from me."

"I see," Deborah said. "You feel like a failure, alone and lost, without any connection in a city you scorn."

"I wouldn't say scorn," Ellie stood. "I don't really feel anything about the city. It's the river I care about."

"Your connection to home," Deborah said.

"Yes," Ellie began walking to the river, "and freedom."

"Ellie?" Deborah stood in shock. "Ellie, what are you talking about?" Ellie continued to walk toward the river, a slow pace. "Ellie, what are you doing?"

Ellie stepped into the Charles, its cool touch chilling her feet. "Going home." She waded deeper.

"Ellie! No!" Deborah ran to the riverbank, digging in her bag for her cell phone.

Ellie stood waist deep in the water when she turned to face her therapist. She smiled, a wild and determined look in her eyes. "Deborah, this must be done. I have to go home."

Slowly, she tilted back, eyes closed, arms spread and let the river embrace her. She could hear Deborah's scream, muffled through the water. She let herself relax and float away.

She saw all the times that she sat on that rotted log with her father, poles in hand, her young imagination running wild with his tales. In each scene, she saw what she never did at the time. A head, just out of the water, beautiful blue-green face smiling benignly, dappled in sun and shade. It had always been at the edge of vision, never registering until this moment as the Charles wrapped her and pushed her downriver.

She saw it now, swimming along beside her, that beautiful blue-green face, and it was smiling at her still, though perhaps even more so. Ellie felt a deep calmness wash over her akin to when she would visit the river, but this time it was much more solid and real. The creature swam circles around her, its hands and feet webbed, green hair flowing behind it like a cloak.

When it placed its webbed hands on her cheeks, she didn't flinch away and she was surprised at the warmth. She had expected cold clamminess. The creature drifted closer and kissed her.

Ellie saw in her mind's eye the drying up of the little brook and the desperate attempt of the creature to flee and find Ellie. No longer under the creature's protection, her father had succumbed to cancer.

For many years, the nixie searched for Ellie. It traveled countless rivers, streams, brooks, ponds and lakes until it finally found the Charles and felt Ellie's pain keenly. It had called out to Ellie the only way it could. Ellie only knew that the river was safe.

"You lost your home too," Ellie said, unsurprised that she could talk underwater.

The nixie nodded, smiling. It spun in a circle and Ellie smiled for the first time in years.

"We're both home now," she said.

The nixie frowned and shook its head. It pointed at Ellie and then at the surface of the river. It then pointed at itself and spun, arms out like an airplane.

"My home is there," Ellie pointed up, "and yours is here?"

The nixie nodded.

"But, I want to stay with you," Ellie said.

The nixie once again shook its head. It hugged Ellie and she felt then that they could be apart, that the nixie would always be there for her in the river. The nixie placed two webbed fingers on Ellie's eyelids and gently closed Ellie's eyes. She drifted along, supported by the nixie and the river they both loved, for an eternity.

She opened her eyes when she felt a pulsing on her chest. Harsh sunlight glared as she vomited river water. Deborah was there, looking worried, along with paramedics and firemen. A few early morning joggers had stopped to watch and were standing among the ambulance and fire trucks.

"Miss?" the paramedic who had been pushing on her chest asked. "Miss, can you hear me?"

"Yes." Ellie coughed more water.

"What's your name?" he asked.

"Ellie."

"Oh my God! Ellie!" Deborah came running over, dropping to her knees. "I thought you were gone! I thought we lost you!"

"Miss," the paramedic tried to push Deborah away, "we need space."

"Ellie," Deborah said, "are you okay?"

Ellie smiled, feeling the nixie not too far away.

"I will be."

ଓଃଡ

Pythagora Switch

You could see the man with the uncombed brown hair and the wrinkled khakis at the same street corner every day for two years. At 1 o'clock on Monday, he ate a peanut butter sandwich, at 2 o'clock Tuesday he had a donut, and the rest of the week he smoked a cigarette at 3:14. He always stayed on the corner until 4:22 at which point he would sigh loudly, slump his shoulders and shuffle away up Second Street.

He was there every day of the year, no matter the weather and was once featured on the local evening news, though when a reporter asked him some questions, he ignored the woman with the microphone and went about his routine.

From time to time, people said they saw him in other places around town, exhibiting much of the same strange behavior, though those stories were always second or third hand. No one knew his name, where he lived, if he had a job, where he bought groceries. Nobody knew him. He never talked to anyone, never deviated from his routine. In fact, he did not seem to realize that there was an entire world around him.

Children made fun of him, as children do. The teens

were the worst. They called him names, shouted jeers at him, and once, about six months ago, a group of high school kids pushed him down. The man got back up, picked up his donut, and took a bite. Tommy Mason, the school's quarterback, knocked the donut out of his hand and into the street, which caused the teens to begin a whole new take on their name calling. That was the only day the man deviated from his routine. When Tommy knocked the donut away, then man just turned and left, shuffling up Second Street. The high schoolers followed for a bit, but a patrol car came by and they gave up their taunting.

It all ended last week when the most extraordinary thing happened.

It was Wednesday afternoon and the man was smoking a cigarette looking around despondently. He then did something he had never done before. Rather than drop his cigarette at his feet and crush it out, he flicked it into the face of a passing bicyclist. The woman on the bicycle lost control, swerving into a newspaper box, knocking it over. The box crashed open, spilling newspapers at the feet of a father and son who were walking along the sidewalk eating ice cream cones. They both tripped on the newspapers, sending the ice cream to the sidewalk a few feet in front of them. A stray dog burst from an alley, running towards the ruined ice cream, and as it did so, it bumped a trash can that fell into the leg of a fruit stand. The fruit stand toppled over, spilling apples, oranges and melons onto the sidewalk and out into the street. The vendor at the hot dog cart slipped on the apples, jostling his cart. The wheel chuck popped out and the cart rumbled into the street directly into the path of an oncoming SUV whose driver was talking on his cell. The driver hadn't seen the old man crossing the street he was about to hit, but he did see the hot dog cart and slammed down on his brakes, stopping just in time. Cart and old man were safe, and the strange, impromptu Rube Goldberg machine ended.

The man with the uncombed brown hair and the wrinkled khakis glanced at me and smiled sheepishly. Pointing to a bizarre-looking watch on his wrist he said, "The Switch is two years off. I suppose I should have it looked at." Turning, he shuffled away up Second Street.

ঞ

Uncertainty Principle

"I'm not dead, y'know," said a tiny voice from inside the sealed steel box.

Erwin dropped his pencil and jumped out of his chair. The steel box had been sealed shut an hour and a half ago when Erwin had decided to test his theory.

"This cannot be," Erwin mumbled.

"Oh, it can," said the voice. "Are you going to open the box or not? You were supposed to check in on me half an hour ago."

"No," Erwin stared at the box in horror. "You can't be alive or dead," he slowly stretched a hand toward the box. "You shouldn't even be talking."

"And why not?" asked the voice. "At this point in time, I'm both alive and dead. Why can't I talk too?"

"Be quiet! You are not supposed to *be*!"

"When you question reality, Erwin, anything can be," the voice purred.

"I am questioning my sanity at the moment," Erwin mumbled.

"I'm not," the voice sounded amused. "You're the one

that locked a cat in a box with radioactive materials and a bottle of poison."

Erwin fell into his chair, covered his face with both hands and began to weep.

"Crying now, Erwin?" the voice asked. "You should be. This was supposed to be a thought experiment. You weren't actually supposed to do it!"

"I know!" Erwin dropped his hands and shouted at the box. "I know! But they laughed at me. Einstein, Bohr, Heisenberg, the lot of them! The Copenhagen Interpretation has a serious flaw and I only wanted to show them."

The voice was silent for a time. "The Copenhagen Interpretation doesn't apply to everyday objects, Erwin."

"I know that! I wanted only to show that the nature of observation as it applies to the interpretation is not well defined. The wave function collapses at the point of conscious observation." Erwin was pacing now, waving his arms about, frantic to make his point to the voice.

"Erwin, you know what the end result will always be," the voice was angry. "Unconscious observation by a Geiger counter is enough to determine when the wave collapses." The voice paused. "You never had to put me in the box."

"I know," Erwin collapsed toward the table upon which the box sat. Gingerly, he released the catch and opened the lid. Inside, the poison capsule was broken and a cat lay dead.

"What will your daughter say when she finds me missing, Erwin?" the voice accused.

ꕥ

Journal Entry: March 6, 2013

It's a trick, sleight-of-hand, a sham.

At least, that's what I tell myself it should be.

In truth, it's two competing realities: one in my head and the other outside of it. A conflict that carries on daily, one that not even the greatest mediator can resolve.

Inside, it's dark fae, witches, macabre morticians, lost dwarves, trees, dying soldiers, jazz musicians and darkness. They pound the inside of my skull, all shouting at my inner ear their remarkable stories, begging for their tales to be told. Each morning, I pick the one voice that shouts louder than the others and begin transcribing its words. The next day, the lottery renews.

That's how I would like my mornings to go, but the outer reality can be bigger and louder than the inner, often when I don't want it to. In many ways, I'm still a child and would do anything to shirk my duties. But, it is an onus I have put upon myself, a mantle of family that is heavier than any mountain.

So it is that I find myself on this morning, having chosen to listen to Athame describe her encounter with the lily-haired fae, that the outer world slammed me like a battering ram, Athame receding into the dark recesses while I sit reeling from it all.

How do I juggle these dimensions when the inner world is more real than the outer? When I grow angry and frustrated at being torn away from my friends, what should I do?

The daily morning ritual is just that, the time when the gates open is small and once they close, they do not open again until the next day. So many untold stories and the roster grows by the hour.

I wish it could be smoke and mirrors, an illusion of productivity, but most days, there are no words at all.

ೞ

Swing Life Away

Nobody is pretty first thing in the morning. I heard that somewhere and I believe it for true.

We swung away at life, bulling through everything we encountered and survived it all, hitting home runs, but striking out just as much, if not more. There have been births and deaths, wealth and poverty, lucidity and insanity. All wrapped neatly in the mundane.

Prices have been paid and I feel justified in finally following my dreams.

Nobody is pretty first thing in the morning. I heard that somewhere and know it for a lie. Today, she looks like she did ten years ago and I'll keep swinging away with her.

ଔଷ

The Straight Man

"I don't want you to feel bad for me," she said as they walked down L Street under the dim streetlights.

"Might as well say you want me to stop loving you," he responded, noting how she crossed her arms. "Because that's where it comes from, y'know."

"I know," she sighed.

"Look," he pointed to a garish blue sign, the old kind of wooden sign hanging above a doorway. Centered on it was a photographic-quality face of an old woman with snow-white hair pulled into an enormous bun. Gilded letters read *Millie's Tavern.*

"What about it?"

"Let's go in. Grab a few drinks," he shrugged, a smile playing on his lips. "Loosen up and push the bullshit down for a bit."

She stopped and studied the sign. "That has got to be the dumbest sign I have ever seen." She squinted her eyes and stared at it, scrunching her nose. "Nope, doesn't help. Maybe if they got rid of the neon?"

He laughed. "C'mon. The first round's on me."

"Damn right it is," she said. "You haven't taken me out to a bar in over a decade."

He laughed again and made a mock chivalrous show of holding the door open. "M'lady."

It was her turn to laugh as she flipped her hair over her shoulder, straightened her back, and strutted through the doorway.

Inside, Millie's Tavern was dim, as bars usually are—but that was the only usual thing about it. All around was a jumble of miss-matched chairs and tables. The lighting was gas-light, mere flickers of flame throwing weak light on the reflectors. Portraits from the nineteenth century were hung evenly spaced between the gas-light sconces. Along the back wall was a bar, bowed in the center from decades of use. Serving girls rushed about, dressed in old west petticoats and corsets, their breasts pushed as high as their hair, depositing drinks at each table in the form of Mason jars.

"What the fuck?" she asked in shock. "What is this place?"

"I don't know," he said as his eyes followed a server breezing past, "but I'd like to find out."

She pursed her lips. "I'm sure you would."

"No," he said, the "O" drawing out. "It's a weird place. I want to know why."

She nodded and led the way to an empty table.

The arms of the chairs were sticky and the tabletop had the tell-tale signs of being cleaned with a dirty rag. Within seconds, a bouncy redheaded server approached and asked what they wanted.

After ordering, she said, "Aw, she's just your type. Big boobs and red hair."

"What?"

"I saw you ogling her," she laughed. "It's okay. I know I'm nothing much."

He smiled and reached across the table, holding her hand. "You are much more than you realize."

She pulled her hand back, a wicked look in her eye. "I told you, I'm not going to marry you," she said loud enough for the entire bar to hear. "I told you to stop asking."

Head buried in his hands he uttered a muffled, "Geez."

Hours later, as they continued their walk down L Street, holding hands, she smiled up at him.

"You were right," she said. "I do feel better."

"Anything for you," he told her, "Even if I have to be your straight man."

"You're the best husband I ever had," she said as she gave his waist a squeeze.

ଔଔ

The Thirteenth Day

"Thank you, Ma'am! I believe a fellow could get used to this sort of treatment."

"Jack! Don't be silly."

"Don't stop. I need it."

"I can't rub your shoulders all day. My hands already hurt."

"I know, Jackie, but I wish this whole thing was over. We don't know what's going to happen."

"Jack…"

"When that boy was shot down…I…I wanted to shove all we had down Kruschev's throat. Jackie, I'm not that kind of man."

"I know. You're a great man, Jack. You'll do the right thing."

"Mmm. The Joint Chiefs are barking at me constantly. O'Donnell keeps going on about the political ramifications. Bobby…well, Bobby's being Bobby. I hope we're right. Is this what we signed on for? I thought we could do better than all the others. I wanted to make this country great again."

"But you are, Jack. Can't you see? The country looks up

to you."

"Do they? They're people outside right now screaming 'Free Cuba.' Free Cuba? How can I do that? The Soviets have missiles pointed at those people's homes and they want me to leave Cuba alone! It's 1962 for God's sake! Don't they understand? Don't they realize what's at stake?"

"They must. Jack, you can't do this to yourself."

"Can't I? I've sent my answer to Kruschev's deal despite what happened to that pilot, despite our U2 getting lost over Siberia and nearly shot down. If he doesn't accept, it'll be war, Jackie. War! Do you know what that means? War! People will die and it'll be my fault for not having stopped it. I am responsible for every American life out there. Don't tell me I can't do this to myself. How can I live with myself if the worst happens?"

"But it won't, will it, Jack? Kruschev will accept. He has to. He doesn't want this any more than you do. He can't... nobody's that much of a monster."

"I hope you're right, Jackie. I really do. But we're taking a big gamble with this deal. We're not even sure it came from Kruschev in the first place. But if he accepts...Jackie, if he accepts, it'll be over. It'll be over and I'm sure O'Donnell will remind me time and again what a bargaining chip we've gained. Ugh, this whole thing is so vicious."

"Here, Jack. I've got you a drink."

"Thanks."

"Jack, you are the leader of the Free World. You've got a team of really good men working for you. Kenny..."

"Kenny. Kenny O'Donnell's been my friend for 15 years and I feel like he's not behind me one hundred percent on this. Oh, don't get me wrong, he'll support me openly, but I'm not sure what's going on in his head anymore."

"Do you still know what's going on in my head, Jack?"

"Yes, Jackie. The children."

"The children, Jack. You'll do the right thing and everything will be fine because of the children."

"I haven't stopped thinking about them through all this. I keep thinking, 'What kind of world will I leave them if I do the wrong thing?' It's hard, Jackie, damn hard."

"I know."

"This has got to work because if it doesn't, it's war and the children will have nothing."

"What was the deal, Jack?"

"The deal? Mmm…the Soviets agree to dismantle and remove their missiles from Cuba. In return, we don't invade Cuba and we don't help anybody who does. Also…we have to remove the old Jupiter missiles from Turkey."

"Remove our missiles? Jack, what about the politics?"

"The politics. The politics. The Soviets must agree to keep the information about the Jupiters under the table for six months until we can start to remove them. If they don't, we deny everything. We'll come out looking strong if this works."

"Will we?"

"To the rest of the world, yes, we will. Pray to God it works, Jackie. Pray."

"Mr. President? The Attorney General, Admiral Hayes and General May are here to see you, sir."

"Send them in."

"Yes, sir."

"Bobby. Admiral. General. Sit down, will you?"

"Jack, he took it! Kruschev took it! They start removal today."

"Thank God, Bobby. Jackie, did you hear?"

"Yes."

"Admiral, General. Order a stand down. Monday's scheduled invasion is cancelled."

"Yes, Mr. President."

"Yes, sir."

"Bobby, get O'Donnell in here. Jackie, it worked. It worked!"

"Yes, Jack, it did. Oh my God. You did it."

"Yes, we all did. Jackie?"

"Yes?"

"Let's go visit the children."

ꕥ

Angel of the Ardennes
The Ardennes Trilogy, Part 3

At some point, they gave me morphine. The cloud I float on is soft and comforting, but it is bouncing up and down violently. A symphony of bees is living in my ears while muted lights flash on the edges of my vision. I try to tell the bouncing and the bees to stop, but they don't. I'm not even sure I've spoken aloud. I'm not even sure where I am.

I had given up in my attempts for peace and quiet some time before when the noise and bouncing stop. I think I hear voices, but they are far away, filtered through a haze of muddy water.

"…another one!"

"That building there! Hurry!"

The bouncing starts again, and I feel tilted, like my feet are slowly rotating above my head. I try to open my eyes, and the blurry sight is upside down. A green mass is right in front of me and the sky is down. I try to find my feet and after the steel-gray passes my eyes, all I can see is another green mass down by my feet. This one might have a face, but if it does, it's just a fleshy blur.

The dim light of the sky winks out and is replaced by a soft glow. I guess I'm in the building now, but I still don't know where it is. Sleep seems to be a good idea.

Walking patrol between Champs and Longchamps was part of the mobile defense of Bastogne, but Corporal Walker wondered why they couldn't just dig in a slit trench and wait for the Jerrys to show up. It was cold, the locals said it was the coldest winter they could remember, and Walker dreamed of heat, whether it was a hot shower, a campfire or even hot food. More often than not, the rations were frozen solid and Walker and his buddies had to suck on them so that they would melt enough to be chewed. And that was when they had rations. There hadn't been a supply dump in over a week.

There had been some action, mostly along the southern ring of the defense where the 506th and 501st were stationed, but Walker and others of the 502nd PIR hadn't seen any action yet. The officers said that a major Jerry offensive was imminent. Bastogne was surrounded and the 101st Airborne Division was lacking food, ammunition, medical supplies and officers. It was up to men like Walker and Sargent Mulberry to lead the men. That didn't mean Walker had to like it.

It was quiet the morning of December 22nd. Word had come down last night that the Jerrys had all the roads in and out of Bastogne under their jackboots. The Americans were good and caught. Walker had been ordered to take a squad on patrol of the perimeter just east of Champs about five miles and then back again. The men were on edge and so was he. Jones was on point and Walker could just make out his shape trudging through the snow about fifty yards ahead, moving from tree to tree. Jones was a good man, had dropped into Normandy with Walker the night of Operation Overlord.

They had seen a lot together since then and were enjoying a much needed rest when the 101st was called into help with the defense of Bastogne. Walker trusted Jones with his life, who wouldn't, after everything?

Without warning, the rumble of Panzers thundered through the forest. The squad froze and dropped into cover. Walker scanned the trees, a mask of disbelief on his face. It sounded as if the tanks were behind the lines! Jones came trotting back, dropped next to Walker.

"Bob, it sounds like…" Jones cut off when Walker waved a hand.

"Yeah, they got behind us," Walker whispered intently.

"What do we do?" Jones asked, hefting his M-1 rifle as if he intended taking the Panzers on with that alone.

"Didja see how many they are or even what type?"

"Maybe 15 fours," Jones answered while he watched the forest from where the tanks rumbled.

"Panzer IVs?" Walker was incredulous. "All right, we gotta get out of here quick, regroup and report to Lieutenant Cassidy. Hopefully we can stop them before they reach Champs."

Jones nodded. Walker had just hand-signaled to the squad, ordering them back to camp, when the tree next to him exploded. He was thrown to the ground as the Panzers' big guns thundered, raining hot death into his squad. Walker's only thought as he closed his eyes was that Lt. Cassidy had to be warned.

The light wakes me. It's not bright, but it is enough. My legs hurt, pain like I've never had. Maybe I moan, I don't know, but a coffee-colored angel fills my vision then. She speaks but I don't understand her. She's speaking English, I'm sure of it, but her accent is thick with French and African lilts. I don't mind though. She smiles, and that alone makes me forget the pain. Almost.

"Dis will help with the pain," she says as she gives me a morphine shot. I immediately begin to drift.

"You're beautiful," I whisper to her, my words floating from my mouth and hovering between us.

She smiles again, but it is a smile of bedside manner, one that says she has heard those words hundreds of times.

"Sleep now," she murmurs, a hand on my head.

The English day was gray and thick with moisture. Privates Walker and Jones were huddled on empty ammo boxes, a third between them while they played Rummy.

"I hate this waiting," Jones complained. "How many times have we had to get ready only to have the Honchos cancel things?"

"Yeah, I know," Walker laid down a trio of Aces, smiling. "Heh, 15."

"Asshole," Jones mumbled.

"They say the weather is gonna clear," Walker discarded.

"They haven't gotten that right yet have they?" Jones mumbled again as he studied his cards. "Jesus, you're kicking my ass."

"Maybe today's the day."

"Maybe," Jones drew a card and furrowed his brow. "What do you think it'll be like over there? I mean, lotsa Jerrys, sure, but how about the women?" Jones' grin was wicked. "You know what they say about French women."

Walker chuckled. "Yeah, that'd be real nice, huh? Swoop in, rescue some French farm girls from the evil Nazis and their fathers will give them away as a reward to the strong

American soldiers."

They both laughed. "Naw," Jones got out between guffaws, "I want me one of them fancy Paris girls." He laid a finger on the side of his nose. "They know things we can't even dream of."

They both laughed again as the P.A. shouted, "All personnel of the 101st Airborne Division report to Tarmac C for assembly! All personnel of the 101st…"

"That's us," Jones said, throwing down his cards.

"Yep," Walker agreed. "Let's go rescue some farm girls."

The light wakes me once again. It's been five days since they brought me to the hospital. My right leg is gone, amputated by the doctors when they realized it had been too torn up to save. My ticket home once it's safe to transport me there.

Jones and the rest of my squad are dead. I cried when I found out three days ago, weeping alone in the night. The following morning, my angel sat beside me and held my hand. She said she had heard me and offered sympathy. Augusta is her name. She said that she was from the Congo and moved to Belgium when she was a teenager.

She has been spending her free time, what little she has, with me. We talk of our childhoods and our dreams. We both know that this friendship will never last, but we cling to each other in the center of this Belgian hell, each taking from the other strength to continue. Her eyes are as haunted as mine and she prefers to talk of happier times, as do I.

On this fifth day, she helps me into a chair and we go outside among the rubble to enjoy much needed fresh air away from the sounds and smells of death. It's still cold, but the freeze that gripped the Ardennes has lifted. We sit quietly for a time, enjoying the silence. I ask her why it's quiet and she smiles in that special way she reserves just for me, the way she did on that morning she first comforted me, and hands me a small package wrapped in an old newspaper.

"Merry Christmas," she says.

"It's Christmas?" I ask in surprise. "I had no idea."

She points to the package. "Open it."

I tear the paper off gleefully, an innocent happiness bubbling in my chest. It's a matchbox and when I slide it open, I see inside an ugly piece of metal.

"What's this?" I ask, revulsion twisting my chest.

"It is the shrapnel the doctor took from the leg he could save," she whispers.

"Why?" I am aghast at this gift. "Why would you give this to me?"

"Because, it will be a reminder of what you have lost," she says slowly, "but it is also a reminder of what was saved." She sighs. "It is also a reminder of what can never be."

I look at her then. "What, Augusta?" I hold her hand, imploring. "What can never be?"

Tears silently roll down her cheeks. "Us, Robert. We can never be." She buries her face in her hands, sobs rocking her. "We can never truly be friends. Not here. Not in this time or place, no matter how much we may want it."

She leaves then, running back to the hospital. I sit alone in the center of Bastogne, Belgium, unable to stand on my own, crying onto an ugly piece of German metal I intend to keep forever.

ঔ

Acknowledgments

As with any book, this one would not have been possible without the help of many people, whether they know it or not, and whether they wanted to or not.

Many of these stories would never have been written if not for writing prompts I found online. Thanks to Lance of 100 Word Song, Kelly of Scriptic, Cameron, Angela and Mandy of Write on Edge, Stephanie of Master Class and many others I cannot remember. The time you spend each week hosting writers and encouraging us has been invaluable.

The other three writers of the Fab Four Fable group, David, Shannon and Stephanie, have been wonderful people to me and each other. They have been there for advice, both literary and personal, and their words, too, deserve to be read.

Thanks also to Matt, Rich, Shannon and Tracey who read these stories for me and offered much needed advice. Without it, they would be poor lies, indeed.

A special thanks to Marian (with an "A"), who took a chance on an unpublished writer, encouraging me to produce the book you now hold with a very firm, "Give me more words, Mister!"

And, of course, my family, living in many houses in New Hampshire, New York and Rhode Island. Your encouragement and support these past years while I have been a horror to deal with, have made this possible. I am forever in your debt.

words, Mister!"

And, of course, my family, living in many houses in New Hampshire, New York and Rhode Island. Your encouragement and support these past years while I have been a horror to deal with, have made this possible. I am forever in your debt.

Made in the USA
Charleston, SC
15 October 2013